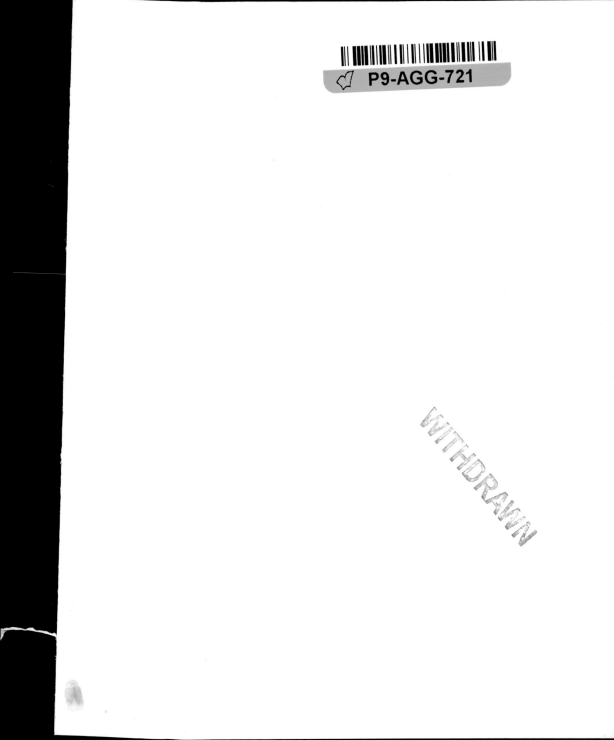

Who Feels Surprised, Dear Dragon?

by Margaret Hillert

Illustrated by Jack Pullan

NORWOOD HOUSE PRESS

DEAR CAREGIVER,

The *Beginning-to-Read* series is comprised of carefully written books that extend the collection of classic readers you may remember from your own childhood. Each book features text comprised of common sight words to provide your child ample practice reading the words that appear most frequently in written text. The many additional details in the pictures enhance the story and offer the opportunity for you to help your child expand oral language and develop comprehension.

Begin by reading the story to your child, followed by letting him or her read familiar words and soon your child will be able to read the story independently. At each step of the way, be sure to praise your reader's efforts to build his or her confidence as an independent reader. Discuss the pictures and encourage your child to make connections between the story and his or her own life. At the end of the story, you will find reading activities and a word list that will help your child practice and strengthen beginning reading skills.

Above all, the most important part of the reading experience is to have fun and enjoy it!

Shannon Cannon

Shannon Cannon, Ph.D., Literacy Consultant

Norwood House Press • P.O. Box 316598 • Chicago, Illinois 60631
For more information about Norwood House Press please visit our website at
www.norwoodhousepress.com or call 866-565-2900.

LIBRARY OF CONGRESS CATALOGING-IN-PUBLICATION DATA
Names: Hillert, Margaret, author. | Pullan, Jack, illustrator.
Title: Who feels surprised, Dear Dragon? / by Margaret Hillert ; illustrated by Jack Pullan.
Description: Chicago, IL : Norwood House Press, [2017] | Series: A beginning-to-read book | Summary: "A boy, with his pet dragon, find unexpected surprises in a day full of disappointments. This title includes reading activities and a word list"-- Provided by publisher.
Identifiers: LCCN 2016052219 (print) | LCCN 2017014193 (ebook) | ISBN 9781684040087 (eBook) | ISBN 9781599538259 (library edition : alk. paper)
Subjects: | CYAC: Surprise--Fiction. | Rain and rainfall--Fiction. | Dragons--Fiction.
Classification: LCC PZ7.H558 (ebook) | LCC PZ7.H558 Wgx 2017 (print) | DDC [E]--dc23
LC record available at https://lccn.loc.gov/2016052219

Hardcover ISBN: 978-1-59953-825-9   Paperback ISBN: 978-1-68404-003-2

302N—072017
Manufactured in the United States of America in North Mankato, Minnesota.

Father, Father.
Dear Dragon is sad, and so am I.

He is?
You are?
Why are you sad?

We cannot go out and play.
It is wet.
There is rain.

You can play in here.
You can play with Spot.
He likes to play with you.

Oh, yes!
It is fun to play inside with Spot.
What a surprise!

I am sad.
I want my friends.

You cannot play with your friends
in the rain.
But you can read a book.
You can find friends in books too!

Oh yes.
I see many friends in the books.
What a surprise!

Oh, look!
That dragon looks like you.
What a surprise!

Father, Father!
We are sad.

Why are you sad now?

We want something to eat.
Can we have some food?

Yes! Yes!
Let's make cookies.

Look, Father!
This cookie looks like my
friend in the book.

Yes it does.
Now are you sad?

No, no.
We had fun inside today.
I am surprised!

Oh look!
The rain is gone.
What a good surprise!
We can go out and play.

Look what I have for you.

You made us cookies.
What a good surprise!

Here you are with me.
And here I am with you.
Oh what a day of surprises, Dear Dragon.

The following activities support the findings of the National Reading Panel that determined the most effective components for reading instruction are: Phonemic Awareness, Phonics, Vocabulary, Fluency, and Text Comprehension.

Phonemic Awareness: Syllabication

Say the following words, clapping the syllables as you say them. Ask your child to tell you how many syllables are in each word:

Father-2	sad-1	cannot-2	play-1
inside-2	surprise-2	friends-1	books-1
dragon-2	something-2	food-1	cookies-2
here-1	today-2	happy-2	dear-1

Phonics: Syllabication

1. Explain to your child that syllables in words with two consonants together are divided between the consonants. Write the following words on separate index cards:

happy(hap-py)	mommy(mom-my)	little(lit-tle)
dinner(din-ner)	daddy(dad-dy)	pretty(pret-ty)
puddle(pud-dle)	apple(ap-ple)	muddy(mud-dy)
pizza(piz-za)	yellow(yel-low)	sorry(sor-ry)

2. Ask your child to cut (for younger children, ask them to draw a line for you to cut along) the words apart based on the syllables that are divided between the two consonants.

3. Mix the separated word parts up, and help your child put them together to make words.

Vocabulary: Homophones

1. Explain to your child that words that sound the same but have different meanings are called homophones.

2. Write each of the following words on separate pieces of paper: to, too, two.

3. Read the sentences below to your child and ask them to hold up the piece of paper showing the correct homophone that will complete the sentence.

   • I would like _____ cookies. (two)

   • It is _____ wet outside to play. (too)

   • It is fun ____ play inside with Spot. (to)

   • Dear Dragon is sad _____. (too)

   • We would like something _____ eat. (to)

   • I see _____ of my friends! (two)

Fluency: Echo Reading

1. Reread the story to your child at least two more times while your child tracks the print by running a finger under the words as they are read. Ask your child to read the words he or she knows with you.

2. Reread the story, stopping after each sentence or page to allow your child to read (echo) what you have read. Repeat echo reading and let your child take the lead.

Text Comprehension: Discussion Time

1. Ask your child to retell the sequence of events in the story.

2. To check comprehension, ask your child the following questions:

   • Why can't the boy and Dear Dragon go out and play?

   • What does the boy make with his father?

   • Why is the boy surprised on pages 22 and 23?

   • When you can't go out and play, what are your favorite things to do inside?

WORD LIST

Who Feels Surprised, Dear Dragon? uses the 74 words listed below.

The **6** words bolded below serve as an introduction to new vocabulary, while the other 68 are pre-primer. You may wish to write the words on index cards and use them to help your child build automatic word recognition. Regular practice with these words will enhance your child's fluency in reading connected text.

a	eat	had	made	sad	us
am		have	make	see	
and	father	he	many	so	want
are	find	here	me	some	we
	food		my	something	**wet**
book(s)	for	I		spot	what
but	friend(s)	in	no	**surprise**	why
	fun	**inside**	now	**surprised**	with
can		is		**surprises**	
cannot	go	it	of		yes
cookie(s)	gone		oh	that	you
	good	lets	out	the	your
day		like(s)		there	
dear		look(s)	play	this	
does				to	
dragon			rain	today	
			read	too	

Photograph by Glenna Washburn

ABOUT THE AUTHOR Margaret Hillert has helped millions of children all over the world learn to read independently. She was a first grade teacher for 34 years and during that time started writing books that her students could both gain confidence in reading and enjoy. She wrote well over 100 books for children just learning to read. As a child, she enjoyed writing poetry and continued her poetic writings as an adult for both children and adults.

ABOUT THE ILLUSTRATOR A talented and creative illustrator, Jack Pullan, is a graduate of William Jewell College. He has also studied informally at Oxford University and the Kansas City Art Institute. He was mentored by the renowned watercolor artists, Jim Hamil and Bill Amend. Jack's work has graced the pages of many enjoyable children's books, various educational materials, cartoon strips, as well as many greeting cards. Jack currently resides in Kansas.